D0258548

CORK CI
WITHDRA
FROM STOCK

Published by Top That! Publishing plc
Tide Mill Way, Woodbridge, Suffolk, IP12 1AP, UK
www.topthatpublishing.com
Copyright © 2013 Top That! Publishing plc
All rights reserved
0 2 4 6 8 9 7 5 3 1
Printed and bound in China

Creative Director – Simon Couchman
Editorial Director – Daniel Graham

Illustrated by Sam McPhillips
Written by Edward Lear

All rights reserved. No part of this publication may be reproduced, stored in a retrieval system, or transmitted in any form or by any means, electronic, mechanical, photocopying, recording or otherwise, without the prior written permission of the publisher. Neither this book nor any part or any of the illustrations, photographs or reproductions contained in it shall be sold or disposed of otherwise than as a complete book, and any unauthorised sale of such part illustration, photograph or reproduction shall be deemed to be a breach of the publisher's copyright.

ISBN 978-1-78244-064-2

A catalogue record for this book is available from the British Library
Printed and bound in China

the JUMBLIES

by Edward Lear

'For my Mum and Dad, Silkiesue and Robert too x'
Sam McPhillips

They went to sea in a sieve, they did,
In a sieve they went to sea:
In spite of all their friends could say,
On a winter's morn, on a stormy day,
In a sieve they went to sea!

8107699
CORK CITY
LIBRARIES

And when the sieve turned round and round,
And everyone cried, 'You'll all be drowned!'
They called aloud, 'Our sieve ain't big,
But we don't care a button! We don't care a fig!
In a sieve we'll go to sea!'

Far and few, far and few,
Are the lands where the Jumblies live;

Their heads are green, and their hands are blue,
And they went to sea in a sieve.

They sailed away in a sieve, they did,
In a sieve they sailed so fast,
With only a beautiful pea-green veil
Tied with a ribbon by way of a sail,
To a small tobacco-pipe mast;

And everyone said, who saw them go,
'O won't they soon be upset, you know!
For the sky is dark, and the voyage is long,
And happen what may, it's extremely wrong
In a sieve to sail so fast!'

Far and few, far and few,
Are the lands where the Jumblies live;
Their heads are green, and their hands are blue,
And they went to sea in a sieve.

The water it soon came in, it did,
The water it soon came in.
So to keep them dry, they wrapped their feet
In a pinky paper all folded neat,
And they fastened it down with a pin.

And they passed the night in a crockery jar,
And each of them said, 'How wise we are!
Though the sky be dark, and the voyage be long,
Yet we never can think we were rash or wrong,
While round in our sieve we spin!'

Far and few, far and few,
Are the lands where the Jumblies live;

Their heads are green, and their hands are blue,
And they went to sea in a sieve.

And all night long they sailed away;
And when the sun went down,
They whistled and warbled a moony song
To the echoing sound of a coppery gong,
In the shade of the mountains brown.

Far and few, far and few,
Are the lands where the Jumblies live;

'O Timballo! How happy we are,
When we live in a sieve and a crockery jar,
And all night long in the moonlight pale,
We sail away with a pea-green sail,
In the shade of the mountains brown!'

Their heads are green, and their hands are blue,
And they went to sea in a sieve.

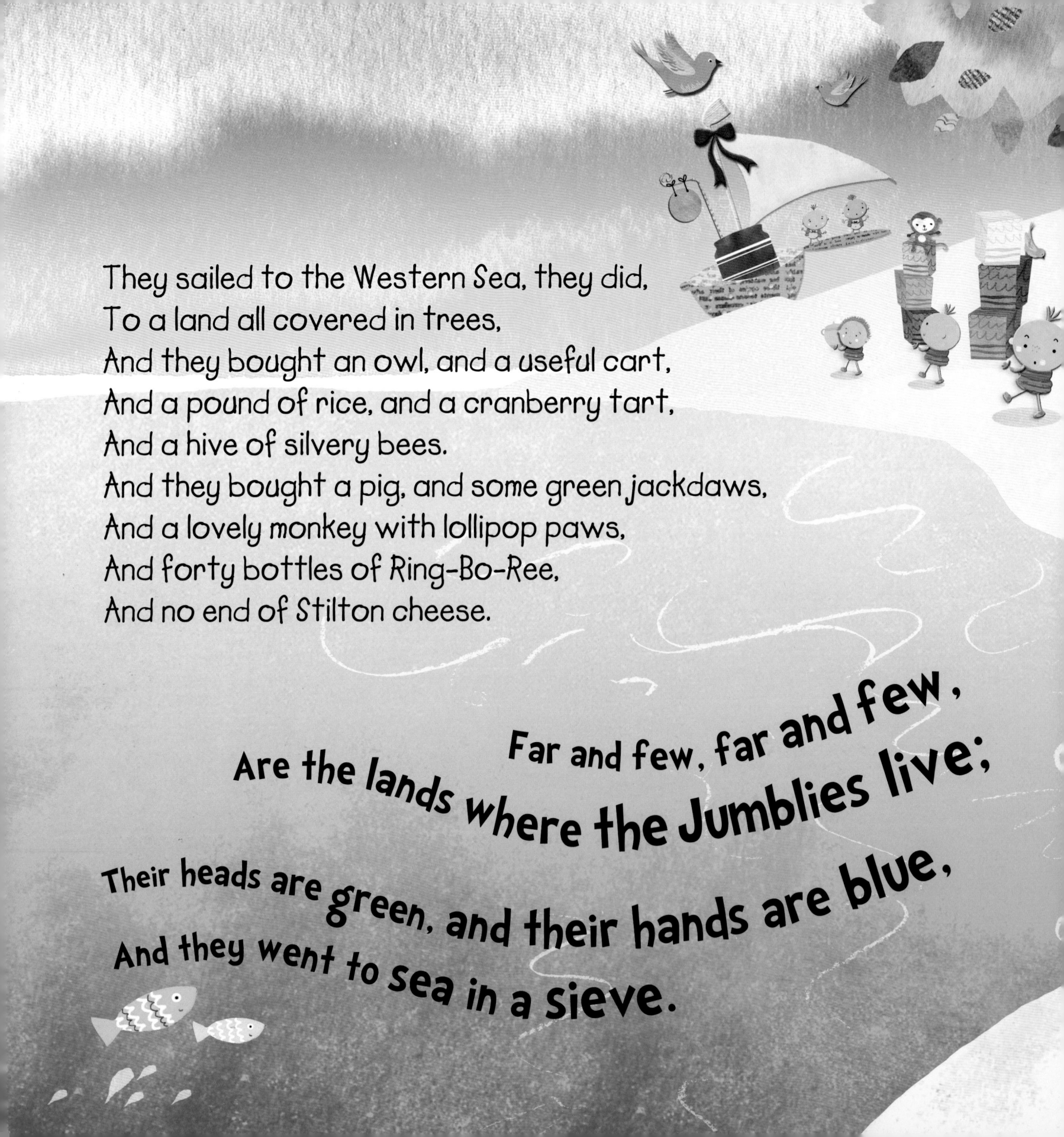

They sailed to the Western Sea, they did,
To a land all covered in trees,
And they bought an owl, and a useful cart,
And a pound of rice, and a cranberry tart,
And a hive of silvery bees.
And they bought a pig, and some green jackdaws,
And a lovely monkey with lollipop paws,
And forty bottles of Ring-Bo-Ree,
And no end of Stilton cheese.

Far and few, far and few,
Are the lands where the Jumblies live;
Their heads are green, and their hands are blue,
And they went to sea in a sieve.

And in twenty years they all came back,
In twenty years or more,
And everyone said, 'How tall they've grown!
For they've been to the Lakes, and the Torrible Zone,
And the hills of the Chankly Bore!'

And they drank their health, and gave them a feast
Of dumplings made of beautiful yeast;
And everyone said, 'If we only live,
We too will go to sea in a sieve,
To the hills of the Chankly Bore!'

WELCOME BACK

YORK CITY LIBRARIES

If you enjoyed this book, then you'll love

'The Quangle Wangle's Hat'

Written by Edward Lear
Illustrated by Sam McPhillips

ISBN 978-1-78244-073-4

This tale, full of fun and folly, recalls the Quangle Wangle and his delightful hat.

ISBN 978-1-84956-610-0

A fox cub experiences his first summer in this heart-warming storybook.

ISBN 978-1-84956-245-4

Unique illustrations capture the loving bond between two best friends!

ISBN 978-1-78244-040-6

Follow the little raindrop's adventure and learn all about the water cycle.

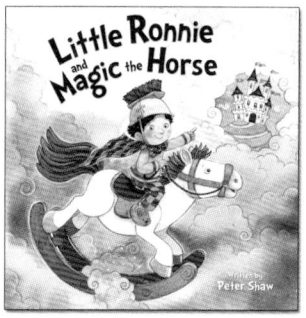

ISBN 978-1-84956-778-7

A fantastical tale about a boy and the adventures he has with his rocking horse.

ISBN 978-1-78244-074-1

Cammy the colourful Chameleon learns an important lesson in this vibrant tale.

ISBN 978-1-78244-059-8

Peter's pebbles come to life in this perfectly crafted tale, full of imagination.

ISBN 978-1-84956-424-3

A wise owl refuses to bow to peer pressure in this amusing, rhyming tale.

ISBN 978-1-84956-438-0

A fantastical tale about unruly, morning hair and a mischievous fairy.

Available from all good bookstores or visit www.topthatpublishing.com